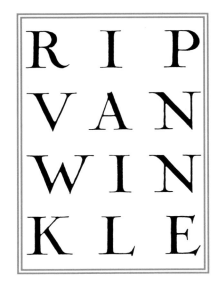

RIP
VAN
WIN
KLE

RIP

WASHINGTON IRVING

VAN

DRAWINGS BY GARY KELLEY

WIN

DESIGN BY LOUISE FILI

KLE

CREATIVE EDITIONS

Illustrations © 1993 Gary Kelley

The text of Rip Van Winkle was written by Washington Irving.

The story was first published in 1820. This edition of Rip Van Winkle was first

published in 1993 by Creative Editions.

Design: Louise Fili

Art Director: Rita Marshall

Design Assistant: Leah Lococo

Published in 1993 by Creative Editions, 123 South Broad Street,

Mankato, Minnesota 56001 USA

Creative Editions is an imprint of Creative Education, Inc.

The publication of this book is a joint venture between

Creative Education, Inc. and American Education Publishing.

PRINTED IN ITALY

LIBRARY OF CONGRESS CATALOGING-IN-PUBLICATION DATA

Irving, Washington, 1783-1859. Rip Van Winkle/written by Washington Irving;

illustrated by Gary Kelley. Summary: A man who sleeps for twenty years in the

Catskill Mountains wakes to a much-changed world.

ISBN 1-56846-082-1

[1. Catskill Mountains Region (N.Y.)—Fiction. 2. New York (State)—Fiction.]

I. Kelley, Gary, ill. II. Title. PZ7.I68Ri 1993

[Fic]—dc20   93-17093

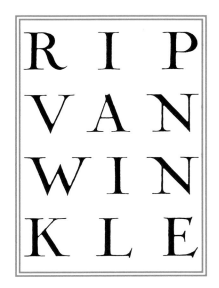

By Woden, God of Saxons,
From whence comes Wensday, that is Wodensday,
Truth is a thing that ever I will keep
Unto thylke day in which I creep into
My sepulchre —

C A R T W R I G H T

THE FOLLOWING TALE WAS FOUND AMONG THE

PAPERS OF THE LATE DIEDRICH KNICKERBOCKER,

AN OLD GENTLEMAN OF NEW YORK, WHO WAS VERY

curious in the Dutch history of the province, and the manners of the

descendants from its primitive settlers. His historical researches, howev-

er, did not lie so much among books as among men; for the former are

lamentably scanty on his favorite topics; whereas he found the old

burghers, and still more their wives, rich in that legendary lore, so

invaluable to true history. Whenever, therefore, he happened upon a

genuine Dutch family, snugly shut up in its low-roofed farmhouse,

under a spreading sycamore, he looked upon it as a little clasped volume

of black-letter, and studied it with the zeal of a book-worm.

The result of all these researches was a history of the province during the

reign of the Dutch governors, which he published some years since.

There have been various opinions as to the literary character of his work, and, to tell the truth, it is not a whit better than it should be. Its chief merit is its scrupulous accuracy, which indeed was a little questioned on its first appearance, but has since been completely established; and it is now admitted into all historical collections, as a book of unquestionable authority. ❧ The old gentleman died shortly after the publication of his work, and now that he is dead and gone, it cannot do much harm to his memory to say that his time might have been much better employed in weightier labors. He, however, was apt to ride his hobby his own way; and though it did now and then kick up the dust a little in the eyes of his neighbors, and grieve the spirit of some friends, for whom he felt the truest deference and affection; yet his errors and follies are remembered "more in sorrow than in anger," and it begins to be suspected, that he never intended to injure or offend. But however his memory may be appreciated by critics, it is still held dear by many folks, whose good opinion is well worth having; particularly by certain biscuit-bakers, who have gone so far as to imprint his likeness on their new-year cakes; and have thus given him a chance for immortality, almost equal to the being stamped on a Waterloo Medal, or a Queen Anne's Farthing.

W HOEVER HAS MADE A VOYAGE UP THE HUDSON MUST REMEMBER THE KAATSKILL MOUNTAINS. They are a dismembered branch of the great Appalachian family, and are seen away to the west of the river, swelling up to a noble height, and lording it over the surrounding country. Every change of season, every change of weather, indeed, every hour of the day, produces some change in the magical hues and shapes of these mountains, and they are regarded by all the good wives, far and near, as perfect barometers. When the weather is fair and settled, they are clothed in blue and purple, and print

their bold outlines on the clear evening sky; but, sometimes, when the

rest of the landscape is cloudless, they will gather a hood of gray vapors

about their summits, which, in the last rays of the setting sun, will glow

and light up like a crown of glory. ❧ At the foot of these fairy

mountains, the voyager may have descried the light smoke curling up

from a village, whose shingle-roofs gleam among the trees, just where the

blue tints of the upland melt away into the fresh green of the nearer land-

scape. It is a little village of great antiquity, having been founded by some

of the Dutch colonists, in the early times of the province, just about the

beginning of the government of the good Peter Stuyvesant (may he rest

in peace!), and there were some of the houses of the original settlers

standing within a few years, built of small yellow bricks brought from

Holland, having latticed windows and gable fronts, surmounted with

weather-cocks. ❧ In that same village, and in one of these very

houses (which, to tell the precise truth, was sadly time-worn and weath-

erbeaten), there lived many years since, while the country was yet a

province of Great Britain, a simple good-natured fellow of the name of

Rip Van Winkle. He was a descendant of the Van Winkles who fig-

ured so gallantly in the chivalrous days of Peter Stuyvesant, and accompanied him to the siege of Fort Christina. He inherited, however, but

little of the martial character of his ancestors. I have observed that he was

a simple good-natured man; he was, moreover, a kind neighbor, and an

obedient hen-pecked husband. Indeed, to the latter circumstance might

be owing that meekness of spirit which gained him such universal popu-

larity; for those men are most apt to be obsequious and conciliating

abroad, who are under the discipline of shrews at home. Their tempers,

doubtless, are rendered pliant and malleable in the fiery furnace of domes-

tic tribulation; and a curtain lecture is worth all the sermons in the world

for teaching the virtues of patience and long-suffering. A termagant wife

may, therefore, in some respects, be considered a tolerable blessing; and

if so, Rip Van Winkle was thrice blessed. ⟩≍⟨ Certain it is that

he was a great favorite among all the good wives of the village, who, as usual, with the amiable sex, took his part in all family squabbles; and never failed, whenever they talked those matters over in their evening gossipings, to lay all the blame on Dame Van Winkle. The children of the village, too, would shout with joy whenever he approached. He assisted at their sports, made their playthings, taught them to fly kites and shoot marbles, and told them long stories of ghosts, witches, and Indians. Whenever he went dodging about the village, he was surrounded by a troop of them, hanging on his skirts, clambering on his back, and playing a thousand tricks on him with impunity; and not a dog would bark at him throughout the neighborhood. The great error in Rip's composition was an insuperable aversion to all kinds of profitable labor. It could not be from the want of assiduity or perseverance; for he would sit on a wet rock, with a rod as long and heavy as a Tartar's lance, and fish all day without a murmur, even though he should not be encouraged by a single nibble. He would carry a fowling-piece on his shoulder for hours together, trudging through woods and swamps, and up hill and down dale, to shoot a few squirrels or wild pigeons. He would never refuse to assist a neighbor even in the roughest

toil, and was a foremost man at all country frolics for husking Indian

corn, or building stone-fences; the women of the village, too, used to

employ him to run their errands, and to do such little odd jobs as their

less obliging husbands would not do for them. In a word Rip was ready

to attend to anybody's business but his own; but as to doing family duty,

and keeping his farm in order, he found it impossible. ⌇⌇ In fact,

he declared it was of no use to work on his farm; it was the most pestilent

little piece of ground in the whole country; every thing about it went

wrong, and would go wrong, in spite of him. His fences were continu-

ally falling to pieces; his cow would either go astray, or get among the

cabbages; weeds were sure to grow quicker in his fields than anywhere

else; the rain always made a point of setting in just as he had some out-

door work to do; so that though his patrimonial estate had dwindled

away under his management, acre by acre, until there was little more left

than a mere patch of Indian corn and potatoes, yet it was the worst con-

ditioned farm in the neighborhood. ⌇⌇ His children, too, were

as ragged and wild as if they belonged to nobody. His son Rip, an

urchin begotten in his own likeness, promised to inherit the habits, with

the old clothes of his father. He was generally seen trooping like a colt

at his mother's heels, equipped in a pair of his father's cast-off galli-

gaskins, which he had much ado to hold up with one hand, as a fine lady

does her train in bad weather. ❧ Rip Van Winkle, however,

was one of those happy mortals, of foolish, well-oiled dispositions, who

take the world easy, eat white bread or brown, whichever can be got with

least thought or trouble, and would rather starve on a penny than work

for a pound. If left to himself, he would have whistled life away in per-

fect contentment; but his wife kept continually dinning in his ears about

his idleness, his carelessness, and the ruin he was bringing on his fami-

ly. Morning, noon, and night, her tongue was incessantly going, and

everything he said or did was sure to produce a torrent of household elo-

quence. Rip had but one way of replying to all lectures of the kind, and

that, by frequent use, had grown into a habit. He shrugged his shoul-

ders, shook his head, cast up his eyes, but said nothing. This, howev-

er, always provoked a fresh volley from his wife; so that he was fain to

draw off his forces, and take to the outside of the house—the only side

which, in truth, belongs to a hen-pecked husband. ❧ Rip's sole

domestic adherent was his dog Wolf, who was as much hen-pecked as

his master; for Dame Van Winkle regarded them as companions in idleness, and even looked upon Wolf with an evil eye, as the cause of his

master's going so often astray. True it is, in all points of spirit befit-

ting an honorable dog, he was as courageous an animal as ever scoured

the woods—but what courage can withstand the ever-during and all-beset-

ting terrors of a woman's tongue? The moment Wolf entered the house

his crest fell, his tail drooped to the ground, or curled between his legs,

he sneaked about with a gallows air, casting many a sidelong glance at

Dame Van Winkle, and at the least flourish of a broomstick or ladle,

he would fly to the door with yelping precipitation.   Times

grew worse and worse with Rip Van Winkle as years of matrimony

rolled on; a tart temper never mellows with age, and a sharp tongue is the

only edged tool that grows keener with constant use. For a long while he

used to console himself, when driven from home, by frequenting a kind

of perpetual club of the sages, philosophers, and other idle personages of

the village; which held its sessions on a bench before a small inn, desig-

nated by a rubicund portrait of His Majesty George the Third. Here

they used to sit in the shade through a long lazy summer's day, talking

listlessly over village gossip, or telling endless sleepy stories about noth-

ing. But it would have been worth any statesman's money to have heard the profound discussions that sometimes took place, when by chance an

old newspaper fell into their hands from some passing traveller. How

solemnly they would listen to the contents, as drawled out by Derrick

Van Bummel, the schoolmaster, a dapper learned little man, who was

not to be daunted by the most gigantic word in the dictionary; and how

sagely they would deliberate upon public events some months after they

had taken place. ⟩⟨ The opinions of this junto were completely

controlled by Nicholas Vedder, a patriarch of the village, and landlord

of the inn, at the door of which he took his seat from morning till night,

just moving sufficiently to avoid the sun and keep in the shade of a large

tree; so that the neighbors could tell the hour by his movements as accu-

rately as by a sun-dial. It is true he was rarely heard to speak, but smoked his pipe incessantly. His adherents, however (for every great man has his adherents), perfectly understood him, and knew how to gather his opinions. When any thing that was read or related displeased him, he was observed to smoke his pipe vehemently, and to send forth short, frequent and angry puffs; but when pleased, he would inhale the smoke slowly and tranquilly, and emit it in light and placid clouds; and sometimes, taking the pipe from his mouth, and letting the fragrant vapor curl about his nose, would gravely nod his head in token of perfect approbation. From even this stronghold the unlucky Rip was at length routed by his termagant wife, who would suddenly break in upon the tranquillity of the assemblage and call the members all to naught; nor was that august personage, Nicholas Vedder himself, sacred from the daring tongue of this terrible virago, who charged him outright with encouraging her husband in habits of idleness. Poor Rip was at last reduced almost to despair; and his only alternative, to escape from the labor of the farm and clamor of his wife, was to take gun in hand and stroll away into the woods. Here he would sometimes seat himself at the foot of a tree, and share the contents of his wallet with Wolf, with whom he sympathized as a fellow-sufferer in persecution. "Poor Wolf," he would say, "thy mistress leads thee a dog's life of it; but never mind, my lad, whilst I live thou shalt never want a friend to stand by thee!" Wolf would wag his tail, look wistfully in his master's face, and if dogs can feel pity I verily believe he reciprocated the sentiment with all his heart.

In a long ramble of the kind on a fine autumnal day, Rip had unconsciously scrambled to one of the highest parts of the Kaatskill mountains. He was after his favorite sport of squirrel shooting, and the still solitudes had echoed and re-echoed with the reports of his gun. Panting and fatigued, he threw himself, late in the afternoon, on a green knoll, covered with mountain herbage, that crowned the brow of a precipice. From an opening between the trees he could overlook all the lower country for many a mile of rich woodland. He saw at a distance the lordly Hudson, far, far below him, moving on its silent but majestic course, with the reflection of a purple cloud, or the sail of a lagging bark, here and there sleeping on its glassy bosom, and at last losing itself in the blue highlands. On the other side he looked down into a deep mountain glen, wild, lonely, and shagged, the bottom filled with fragments from the impending cliffs, and scarcely lighted by the reflected rays of the setting sun. For some time Rip lay musing on this scene; evening was gradually advancing; the mountains began to throw their long blue shadows over the valleys; he saw that it would be dark long before he could reach the village, and he heaved a heavy sigh when he thought of encountering the terrors of Dame Van Winkle.   As he was about to descend, he heard a voice from a distance, hallooing, "Rip Van Winkle! Rip Van Winkle!" He looked round, but could see nothing but a crow winging its solitary flight across the mountain. He thought his fancy must have deceived him, and turned again to descend, when he heard the same cry ring through the still evening air; "Rip Van Winkle! Rip Van Winkle!"—at the same time Wolf bristled up his back, and giving a low growl, skulked to his master's side, looking fearfully down into the glen. Rip now felt a vague apprehension stealing over him; he looked anxiously in the same direction, and perceived a strange figure slowly toiling up the rocks, and bending under the weight of something he carried on his back. He was surprised to see any human being in this lonely and unfrequented place, but supposing it to be some one of the neighborhood in need of his assistance, he hastened down to yield it.   On nearer approach he was still more surprised at the singularity of the stranger's appearance. He was a short square-built old fellow, with thick bushy

hair, and a grizzled beard. His dress was of the antique Dutch fashion—

a cloth jerkin strapped round the waist—several pair of breeches, the outer

one of ample volume, decorated with rows of buttons down the sides, and

bunches at the knees. He bore on his shoulder a stout keg, that seemed

full of liquor, and made signs for Rip to approach and assist him with the

load. Though rather shy and distrustful of this new acquaintance, Rip

complied with his usual alacrity; and mutually relieving one another, they

clambered up a narrow gully, apparently the dry bed of a mountain tor-

rent. As they ascended, Rip every now and then heard long rolling peals,

like distant thunder, that seemed to issue out of a deep ravine, or rather

cleft, between lofty rocks, toward which their rugged path conducted. He

paused for an instant, but supposing it to be the muttering of one of those

transient thunder-showers which often take place in mountain heights, he

proceeded. Passing through the ravine, they came to a hollow, like a small

amphitheatre, surrounded by perpendicular precipices, over the brinks of

which impending trees shot their branches, so that you only caught

glimpses of the azure sky and the bright evening cloud. During the whole

time Rip and his companion had labored on in silence; for though the for-

mer marvelled greatly what could be the object of carrying a keg of liquor up this wild mountain, yet there was something strange and incomprehensible about the unknown, that inspired awe and checked familiarity.

On entering the amphitheatre, new objects of wonder presented themselves. On a level spot in the centre was a company of odd-looking personages playing at nine-pins. They were dressed in a quaint outlandish fashion; some wore short doublets, others jerkins, with long knives in their belts, and most of them had enormous breeches, of similar style with that of the guide's. Their visages, too, were peculiar: one had a large beard, broad face, and small piggish eyes: the face of another seemed to consist entirely of nose, and was surmounted by a white sugar-loaf hat set off with a little red cock's tail. They all had beards, of various shapes and colors. There was one who seemed to be the commander. He was a stout old gentleman, with a weatherbeaten countenance; he wore a laced doublet, broad belt and hanger, high-crowned hat and feather, red stockings, and high-heeled shoes, with roses in them. The whole group reminded Rip of the figures in an old Flemish painting, in the parlor of Dominie Van Shaick, the village parson, and which had been brought over from Holland at the time of the settlement. What seemed particularly odd to Rip was, that though these folks were evi-

dently amusing themselves, yet they maintained the gravest faces, the most

mysterious silence, and were, withal, the most melancholy party of plea-

sure he had ever witnessed. Nothing interrupted the stillness of the scene

but the noise of the balls, which, whenever they were rolled, echoed along

the mountains like rumbling peals of thunder. ❧ As Rip and his

companion approached them, they suddenly desisted from their play, and

stared at him with such fixed statue-like gaze, and such strange, uncouth,

lack-lustre countenances, that his heart turned within him, and his knees

smote together. His companion now emptied the contents of the keg into

large flagons, and made signs to him to wait upon the company. He

obeyed with fear and trembling; they quaffed the liquor in profound

silence, and then returned to their game. ❧ By degrees Rip's

awe and apprehension subsided. He even ventured, when no eye was

fixed upon him, to taste the beverage, which he found had much of the

flavor of excellent Hollands. He was naturally a thirsty soul, and was

soon tempted to repeat the draught. One taste provoked another; and

he reiterated his visits to the flagon so often that at length his senses were

overpowered, his eyes swam in his head, his head gradually declined,

and he fell into a deep sleep. ❧

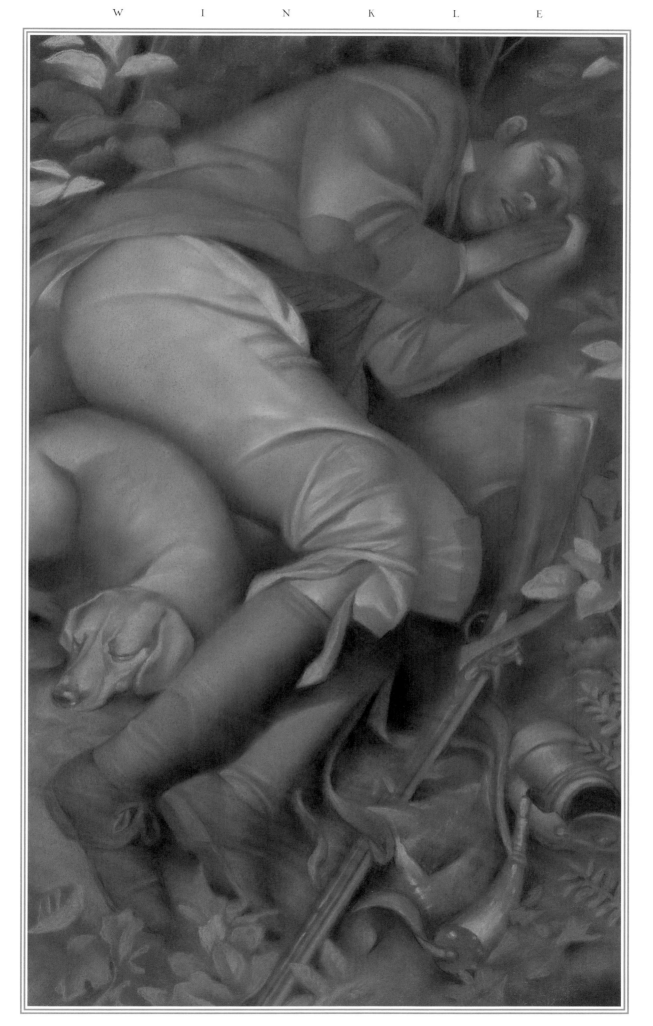

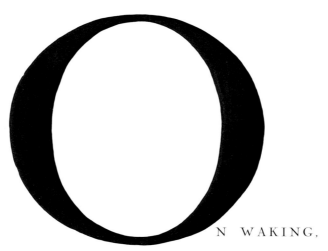N WAKING, HE

FOUND HIMSELF ON THE GREEN KNOLL WHENCE

HE HAD FIRST SEEN THE OLD MAN OF THE GLEN.

He rubbed his eyes—it was a bright sunny morning. The birds were

hopping and twittering among the bushes, and the eagle was wheeling

aloft, and breasting the pure mountain breeze. "Surely," thought Rip,

"I have not slept here all night." He recalled the occurrences before he

fell asleep. The strange man with a keg of liquor—the mountain ravine—

the wild retreat among the rocks—the woebegone party at nine-pins—the

flagon—"Oh! that flagon! that wicked flagon!" thought Rip—"what excuse shall I make to Dame Van Winkle!" ❧ He looked round for his gun, but in place of the clean well-oiled fowling-piece, he found an old firelock lying by him, the barrel incrusted with rust, the lock falling off, and the stock worm-eaten. He now suspected that the grave roysters of the mountain had put a trick upon him, and, having dosed him with liquor, had robbed him of his gun. Wolf, too, had disappeared, but he might have strayed away after a squirrel or partridge. He whistled after him and shouted his name, but all in vain; the echoes repeated his whistle and shout, but no dog was to be seen. ❧ He determined to revisit the scene of the last evening's gambol, and if he met with any of the party, to demand his dog and gun. As he rose to walk, he found himself stiff in the joints, and wanting in his usual activity. "These mountain beds do not agree with me," thought Rip, "and if this frolic should lay me up with a fit of the rheumatism, I shall have a blessed time with Dame Van Winkle." With some difficulty he got down into the glen: he found the gully up which he and his companion had ascended the preceding evening; but to his astonishment a mountain stream was now foaming down it, leaping from rock to rock, and filling the glen with babbling murmurs. He, however, made shift to scramble

up its sides, working his toilsome way through thickets of birch, sas-
safras, and witch-hazel, and sometimes tripped up or entangled by the
wild grapevines that twisted their coils or tendrils from tree to tree, and
spread a kind of network in his path. ❧ At length he reached to
where the ravine had opened through the cliffs to the amphitheatre; but
no traces of such opening remained. The rocks presented a high impen-
etrable wall over which the torrent came tumbling in a sheet of feathery
foam, and fell into a broad deep basin, black from the shadows of the surrounding forest. Here, then, poor Rip was brought to a stand. He
again called and whistled after his dog; he was only answered by the caw-
ing of a flock of idle crows, sporting high in the air about a dry tree that
overhung a sunny precipice; and who, secure in their elevation, seemed
to look down and scoff at the poor man's perplexities. What was to be
done? the morning was passing away, and Rip felt famished for want of
his breakfast. He grieved to give up his dog and gun; he dreaded to meet
his wife; but it would not do to starve among the mountains. He shook
his head, shouldered the rusty firelock, and, with a heart full of trouble
and anxiety, turned his steps homeward. ❧ As he approached
the village he met a number of people, but none whom he knew, which

somewhat surprised him, for he had thought himself acquainted with every one in the country round. Their dress, too, was of a different fashion from that to which he was accustomed. They all stared at him with equal marks of surprise, and whenever they cast their eyes upon him, invariably stroked their chins. The constant recurrence of this gesture induced Rip, involuntarily, to do the same, when, to his astonishment, he found his beard had grown a foot long! He had now entered the skirts of the village. A troop of strange children ran at his heels, hooting after him, and pointing at his gray beard. The dogs, too, not one of which he recognized for an old acquaintance, barked at him as he passed. The very village was altered; it was larger and more populous. There were rows of houses which he had never seen before, and those which had been his familiar haunts had disappeared. Strange names were over the doors—strange faces at the windows—every thing was strange. His mind now misgave him; he began to doubt whether both he and the world around him were not bewitched. Surely this was his native village, which he had left but the day before. There stood the Kaatskill mountains—there ran the silver Hudson at a distance—there was every hill and dale precisely as it had always been—Rip was sorely perplexed—

"That flagon last night," thought he, "has addled my poor head sadly!" ❧❧ It was with some difficulty that he found the way to his own house, which he approached with silent awe, expecting every moment to hear the shrill voice of Dame Van Winkle. He found the house gone to decay—the roof fallen in, the windows shattered, and the doors off the hinges. A half-starved dog that looked like Wolf was skulking about it. Rip called him by name, but the cur snarled, showed his teeth, and passed on. This was an unkind cut indeed—"My very dog," sighed poor Rip, "has forgotten me!" ❧❧ He entered the house, which, to tell the truth, Dame Van Winkle had always kept in neat order. It was empty, forlorn, and apparently abandoned. This desolateness overcame all his connubial fears—he called loudly for his wife and children—the lonely chambers rang for a moment with his voice, and then all again was silence. ❧❧ He now hurried forth, and hastened to his old resort, the village inn—but it too was gone. A large rickety wooden building stood in its place, with great gaping windows, some of them broken and mended with old hats and petticoats, and over the door was painted, "the Union Hotel, by Jonathan Doolittle." Instead of the great tree that used to shelter the quiet little Dutch inn of yore, there now

was reared a tall naked pole, with something on the top that looked like

a red night-cap, and from it was fluttering a flag, on which was a singu-

lar assemblage of stars and stripes—all this was strange and incompre-

hensible. He recognized on the sign, however, the ruby face of King

George, under which he had smoked so many a peaceful pipe; but even

this was singularly metamorphosed. The red coat was changed for one of

blue and buff, a sword was held in the hand instead of a sceptre, the head

was decorated with a cocked hat, and underneath was painted in large

characters, General Washington. There was, as usual, a crowd of folk

about the door, but none that Rip recollected. The very character of the

people seemed changed. There was a busy, bustling, disputatious tone

about it, instead of the accustomed phlegm and drowsy tranquillity. He looked in vain for the sage Nicholas Vedder, with his broad face, dou-

ble chin, and fair long pipe, uttering clouds of tobacco-smoke instead

of idle speeches; or Van Bummel, the schoolmaster, doling forth the

contents of an ancient newspaper. In place of these, a lean, bilious-

looking fellow, with his pockets full of handbills, was haranguing vehe-

mently about rights of citizens—elections—members of congress—liberty—

Bunker's Hill—heroes of seventy-six—and other words, which were a

perfect Babylonish jargon to the bewildered Van Winkle.

The appearance of Rip, with his long grizzled beard, his rusty fowling-

piece, his uncouth dress, and an army of women and children at his

heels, soon attracted the attention of the tavern politicians. They crowd-

ed round him, eyeing him from head to foot with great curiosity. The

orator bustled up to him, and, drawing him partly aside, inquired "on

which side he voted?" Rip stared in vacant stupidity. Another short but

busy little fellow pulled him by the arm, and, rising on tiptoe, inquired

in his ear, "Whether he was Federal or Democrat?" Rip was equally

at a loss to comprehend the question; when a knowing, self-important old

gentleman, in a sharp cocked hat, made his way through the crowd,

putting them to the right and left with his elbows as he passed, and plant-

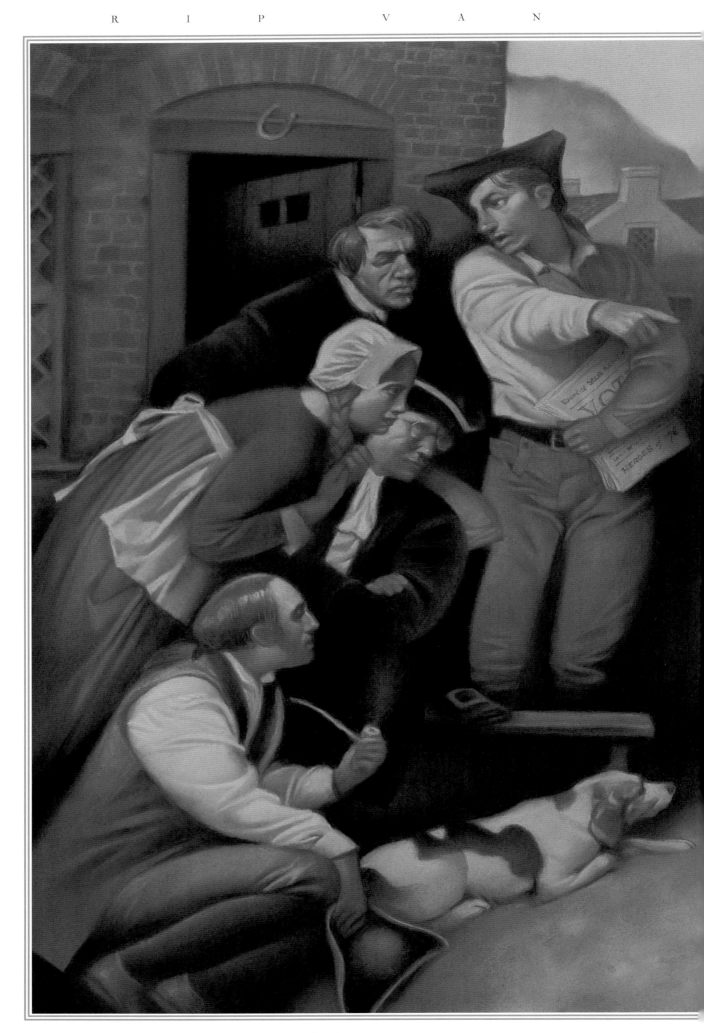

ing himself before Van Winkle, with one arm akimbo, the other resting

on his cane, his keen eyes and sharp hat penetrating, as it were, into his

very soul, demanded in an austere tone, "what brought him to the elec-

tion with a gun on his shoulder, and a mob at his heels, and whether he

meant to breed a riot in the village?"—"Alas! gentlemen," cried Rip,

somewhat dismayed, "I am a poor quiet man, a native of the place, and

a loyal subject of the king, God bless him!"   Here a general

shout burst from the by-standers—"A tory! a tory! a spy! a refugee!

hustle him! away with him!" It was with great difficulty that the self-

important man in the cocked hat restored order; and, having assumed a

tenfold austerity of brow, demanded again of the unknown culprit, what

he came there for, and whom he was seeking? The poor man humbly

assured him that he meant no harm, but merely came there in search

of some of his neighbors, who used to keep about the tavern.

"Well—who are they?—name them."   Rip bethought himself

a moment, and inquired, "Where's Nicholas Vedder?"

There was a silence for a little while, when an old man replied, in a thin

piping voice, "Nicholas Vedder! why, he is dead and gone these eigh-

teen years! There was a wooden tombstone in the church-yard that used to tell all about him, but that's rotten and gone too." ❧

"Where's Brom Dutcher?" ❧ "Oh, he went off to the army in the beginning of the war; some say he was killed at the storming of Stony Point—others say he was drowned in a squall at the foot of Antony's Nose. I don't know—he never came back again." ❧

"Where's Van Bummel, the schoolmaster?" ❧ "He went off to the wars too, was a great militia general, and is now in congress." ❧ Rip's heart died away at hearing of these sad changes in his home and friends, and finding himself thus alone in the world. Every answer puzzled him too, by treating of such enormous lapses of time, and of matters which he could not understand: war—congress—Stony Point— he had no courage to ask after any more friends, but cried out in despair, "Does nobody here know Rip Van Winkle?" ❧ "Oh, Rip Van Winkle!" exclaimed two or three, "Oh, to be sure! that's Rip Van Winkle yonder, leaning against the tree." ❧ Rip looked, and beheld a precise counterpart of himself, as he went up the mountain: apparently as lazy, and certainly as ragged. The poor fellow was now completely confounded. He doubted his own identity, and whether he was himself or another man. In the midst of his bewilderment, the man in the cocked hat demanded who he was, and what was his name?

❧   "God knows," exclaimed he, at his wit's end; "I'm not myself—I'm somebody else—that's me yonder—no—that's somebody else got into my shoes—I was myself last night, but I fell asleep on the mountain, and they've changed my gun, and every thing's changed, and I'm changed, and I can't tell what's my name, or who I am!"   ❧

The by-standers began now to look at each other, nod, wink significantly, and tap their fingers against their foreheads. There was a whisper, also, about securing the gun, and keeping the old fellow from doing mischief, at the very suggestion of which the self-important man in the cocked hat retired with some precipitation. At this critical moment a fresh comely woman pressed through the throng to get a peep at the gray-beard-ed man. She had a chubby child in her arms, which, frightened at his

looks, began to cry. "Hush, Rip," cried she, "hush, you little fool;

the old man won't hurt you." The name of the child, the air of the

mother, the tone of her voice, all awakened a train of recollections in his

mind. "What is your name, my good woman?" asked he. ❧

"Judith Gardenier." ❧ "And your father's name?" ❧

"Ah, poor man, Rip Van Winkle was his name, but it's twenty years

since he went away from home with his gun, and never has been heard

of since—his dog came home without him; but whether he shot himself,

or was carried away by the Indians, nobody can tell. I was then but a

little girl." ❧ Rip had but one question more to ask; but he put

it with a faltering voice: ❧ "Where's your mother?" ❧

"Oh, she too had died but a short time since; she broke a blood-vessel

in a fit of passion at a New-England peddler." ❧ There was a

drop of comfort, at least, in this intelligence. The honest man could con-

tain himself no longer. He caught his daughter and her child in his arms.

"I am your father!" cried he—"Young Rip Van Winkle once—old Rip

Van Winkle now! Does nobody know poor Rip Van Winkle?"

❧ All stood amazed, until an old woman, tottering out from

among the crowd, put her hand to her brow, and peering under it in his face for a moment, exclaimed, "Sure enough! it is Rip Van Winkle—it is himself! Welcome home again, old neighbor—Why, where have you been these twenty long years?" ⌇⌇ Rip's story was soon told, for the whole twenty years had been to him but as one night. The neighbors stared when they heard it; some were seen to wink at each other, and put their tongues in their cheeks: and the self-important man in the cocked hat, who, when the alarm was over, had returned to the field, screwed down the corners of his mouth, and shook his head—upon which there was a general shaking of the head throughout the assemblage. ⌇⌇ It was determined, however, to take the opinion of old Peter Vanderdonk, who was seen slowly advancing up the road. He was a descendant of the historian of that name, who wrote one of the earliest accounts of the province. Peter was the most ancient inhabitant of the village, and well versed in all the wonderful events and traditions of the neighborhood. He recollected Rip at once, and corroborated his story in the most satisfactory manner. He assured the company that it was a fact, handed down from his ancestor the historian, that the Kaatskill mountains had always been haunted by strange beings. That it was affirmed that the great Hendrick Hudson, the first discoverer of the river

and country, kept a kind of vigil there every twenty years, with his crew

of the Half-moon; being permitted in this way to revisit the scenes of his

enterprise, and keep a guardian eye upon the river, and the great city

called by his name. That his father had once seen them in their old

Dutch dresses playing at nine-pins in a hollow of the mountain; and that

he himself had heard, one summer afternoon, the sound of their balls,

like distant peals of thunder.   To make a long story short, the

company broke up, and returned to the more important concerns of the

election. Rip's daughter took him home to live with her; she had a snug,

well-furnished house, and a stout cheery farmer for a husband, whom

Rip recollected for one of the urchins that used to climb upon his back.

As to Rip's son and heir, who was the ditto of himself, seen leaning

against the tree, he was employed to work on the farm; but evinced an

hereditary disposition to attend to any thing else but his business.

  Rip now resumed his old walks and habits; he soon found

many of his former cronies, though all rather the worse for the wear and

tear of time; and preferred making friends among the rising generation,

with whom he soon grew into great favor.   Having nothing to do at home, and being arrived at that happy age when a man can be idle

with impunity, he took his place once more on the bench at the inn door,

and was reverenced as one of the patriarchs of the village, and a chroni-

cle of the old times "before the war." It was some time before he could

get into the regular track of gossip, or could be made to comprehend the

strange events that had taken place during his torpor. How that there

had been a revolutionary war—that the country had thrown off the yoke

of old England—and that, instead of being a subject of his Majesty

George the Third, he was now a free citizen of the United States. Rip,

in fact, was no politician; the changes of states and empires made but lit-

tle impression on him; but there was one species of despotism under

which he had long groaned, and that was—petticoat government.

Happily that was at an end; he had got his neck out of the yoke of mat-

rimony, and could go in and out whenever he pleased, without dreading

the tyranny of Dame Van Winkle. Whenever her name was men-

tioned, however, he shook his head, shrugged his shoulders, and cast up

his eyes; which might pass either for an expression of resignation to his

fate, or joy at his deliverance.   ❧   He used to tell his story to

every stranger that arrived at Mr. Doolittle's hotel. He was observed,

at first, to vary on some points every time he told it, which was, doubtless, owing to his having so recently awaked. It at last settled down precisely to the tale I have related, and not a man, woman, or child in the
neighborhood, but knew it by heart. Some always pretended to doubt the
reality of it, and insisted that Rip had been out of his head, and that this
was one point on which he always remained flighty. The old Dutch

inhabitants, however, almost universally gave it full credit. Even to this
day they never hear a thunderstorm of a summer afternoon about the
Kaatskill, but they say Hendrick Hudson and his crew are at their game
of nine-pins; and it is a common wish of all hen-pecked husbands in the
neighborhood, when life hangs heavy on their hands, that they might
have a quieting draught out of Rip Van Winkle's flagon.

[N O T E]

The foregoing Tale, one would suspect, had been suggested to Mr.
Knickerbocker by a little German superstition about the Emperor
Frederick der Rothbart, and the Kypphaüser mountain: the subjoined
note, however, which he had appended to the tale, shows that it is an
absolute fact, narrated with his usual fidelity: "The story of
Rip Van Winkle may seem incredible to many, but nevertheless I
give it my full belief, for I know the vicinity of our old Dutch settle-
ments to have been very subject to marvellous events and appearances.
Indeed, I have heard many stranger stories than this, in the villages
along the Hudson; all of which were too well authenticated to admit of
a doubt. I have even talked with Rip Van Winkle myself, who,
when last I saw him, was a very venerable old man, and so perfectly
rational and consistent on every other point, that I think no conscien-
tious person could refuse to take this into the bargain; nay, I have seen
a certificate on the subject taken before a country justice and signed with
a cross, in the justice's own handwriting. The story, therefore, is
beyond the possibility of doubt. —D.K."

[P O S T S C R I P T]

The following are travelling notes from a memorandum-book of Mr. Knickerbocker: ✂ The Kaatsberg, or Catskill mountains, have always been a region full of fable. The Indians considered them the abode of spirits, who influenced the weather, spreading sunshine or clouds over the landscape, and sending good or bad hunting seasons. They were ruled by an old squaw spirit, said to be their mother. She dwelt on the highest peak of the Catskills, and had charge of the doors of day and night to open and shut them at the proper hour. She hung up the new moons in the skies, and cut up the old ones into stars. In times of drought, if properly propitiated, she would spin light summer clouds out of cobwebs and morning dew, and send them off from the crest of the mountain, flake after flake, like flakes of carded cotton, to float in the air; until, dissolved by the heat of the sun, they would fall in gentle showers, causing the grass to spring, the fruits to ripen, and the corn to grow an inch an hour. If displeased, however, she would brew up clouds black as ink, sitting in the midst of them like a bottle-bellied spider in the midst of its web; and when these clouds broke, woe betide the valleys! ✂ In old times, say the Indian traditions, there was a kind of Manitou or Spirit, who kept about the wildest recesses of the Catskill Mountains, and took a mischievous pleasure in wreaking all kinds of evils and vexations upon the red men. Sometimes he would assume the form of a bear, a panther, or a deer, lead the bewildered hunter a weary chase through tangled forests and among ragged rocks; and then spring off with a loud ho! ho! leaving him aghast on the brink of a beetling precipice or raging torrent. The favorite abode of this Manitou is still shown. It is a great rock or cliff on the loneliest part of the mountains, and, from the flowering vines which clamber about it, and the wild flowers which abound in its neighborhood, is known by the name of the Garden Rock. Near the foot of it is a small lake, the haunt of the solitary bittern, with water-snakes basking in the sun on the leaves of the pond-lilies which lie on the surface. This place was held in great awe by the Indians, insomuch that the boldest hunter would not pursue his game within its precincts. Once upon a time, however, a hunter who had lost his way, penetrated to the garden rock, where he beheld a number of gourds placed in the crotches of trees. One of these he seized and made off with it, but in the hurry of his retreat he let it fall among the rocks, when a great stream gushed forth, which washed him away and swept him down precipices, where he was dashed to pieces, and the stream made its way to the Hudson, and continues to flow to the present day; being the identical stream known by the name of the Kaaters-kill.